Rocket
Loves
Hide-and-Seek!

All rights reserved. Published in the United States by Schwartz & Wade Books, an imprint of
Random House Children's Books, a division of Penguin Random House LLC, New York.

Schwartz & Wade Books and the colophon are trademarks of Penguin Random House LLC.

Visit us on the Web! rhcbooks.com

Educators and librarians, for a variety of teaching tools, visit us at RHTeachersLibrarians.com

Library of Congress Cataloging-in-Publication Data is available upon request.
ISBN 978-0-593-17792-1 (hardcover) | ISBN 978-0-593-17790-7 (hardcover library binding) |
ISBN 978-0-593-17791-4 (ebook) | ISBN 978-0-593-17789-1 (paperback)

The text of this book is set in 28-point Century.
The illustrations are digitally rendered.

MANUFACTURED IN CHINA
1 2 3 4 5 6 7 8 9 10

Rocket Loves Hide-and-Seek!

Pictures based on the art by Tad Hills

schwartz & wade books • new york

Rocket plays

hide-and-seek.

He looks for Owl
and Bella.

He looks

in a tree.

He looks

under the bushes.

He looks one way.

He looks the other way.

He looks up.

Rocket finds Owl!

"It is my turn to hide,"
says Rocket.

Rocket hides
in the flowers.

Bella finds him

right away.

Rocket hides
behind a tree.

14

Owl finds him
right away.

Rocket hides
in many places.

His friends
find him
every time.

Rocket is sad.

"I am not
a very good hider,"
he says.

"It is just that you
are bigger than us,"
Bella says.

"I have an idea!"

Owl says.

Owl gets leaves.

Bella makes mud.

They cover Rocket
in mud and leaves.

He is ready to hide!

Rocket hides
in the bushes.

Bella does not
find him.

Rocket hides
in a hole.

Rocket loves

hide-and-seek!

Owl does not
find him.

The friends play
together all day.